Mia Learns to Soar

by **Kailanya S. Brailey**

**Illustrations by
Mike Motz**

*This book is dedicated to the greats,
to those who soar...
because that's what eagles do.*

Guess what!
*You can scan the QR code to enjoy
a free audio version of this book!*

Mia Learns to Soar

by Kailanya S. Brailey

Illustrations by
Mike Motz

Mia loves to play dress up
and put outfits together,
to prance around the neighborhood
no matter what the weather.

While her older sister is texting,
phone up to her nose,
Mia is in her closet
admiring her pretty clothes.

Her father is a truck driver
who has to leave before dawn.
By the time she awakes,
he is already gone.

So this morning begins
just like any other –
with the daily fashion show
starring Mia for her mother.

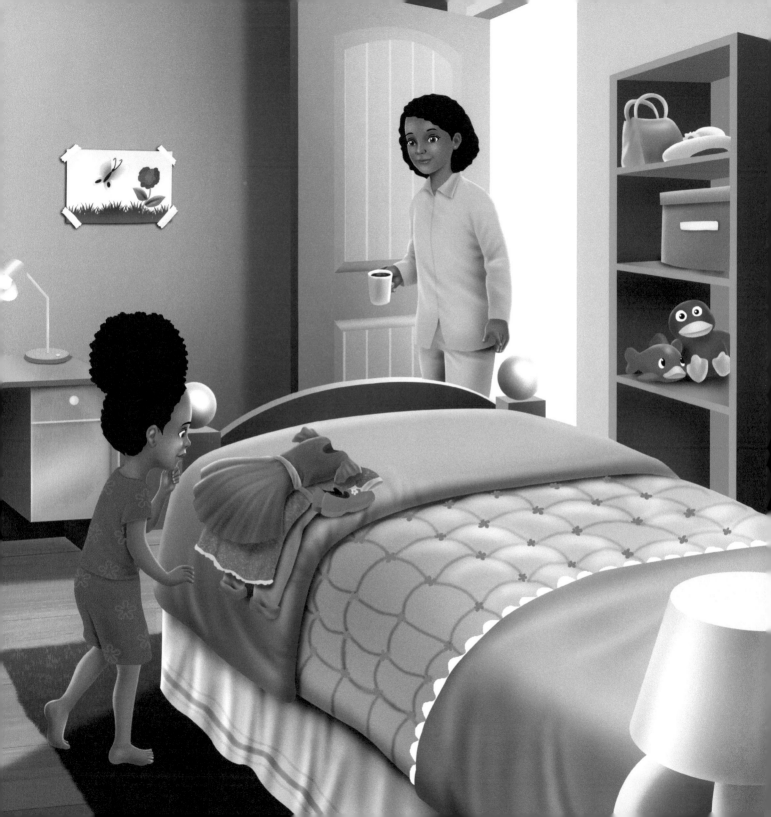

She brings out her shoes,
all the dresses that are there,
for it is never easy
deciding what to wear.

She tries outfit after outfit
until she finds the right one,
then flies downstairs for breakfast
when she is finally done.

And though it is early,
there is lots of conversation
about everything from fashion
to multiplication.

Mia cleans off the table,
which is the family rule.
She kisses her mother goodbye
and heads off to school.

She hops on the bus and
says hello to Ms. Gladys,
her best friend, Jaden,
Alexandra, and Travis.

As the bus leaves the stop,
a smile creeps across Mia's face.
She just cannot wait
to get to her favorite place.

The bus ride is bumpy —
winding roads, lots of trees,
passing fields of corn
that grow up past your knees.

After a few more stops,
they finally enter the gate.
Mia skips to Ms. Johnson's class.
She is never late.

Ms. Johnson stands at her door,
giving students their own greeting.
When everyone is settled,
they circle up for the morning meeting.

All the students sit quietly
to hear what Ms. Johnson has to say.
They listen carefully
as she reads the Question of the Day.

"Students, the future is unknown.
What is to come, we cannot see.
When you grow up,
what do you want to be?

"Some may think it's too early.
Graduation is not near.
But it is never too soon
to start thinking about a career.

"As we go around the circle,
tell what you want to do.
What is that dream job
that you want to come true?"

As the students answer,
Ms. Johnson pays attention
and notices the different careers
they happen to mention.

Some students are future doctors.
Some are lawyers and mayors.
There are future teachers,
singers, and basketball players.

When it is Mia's turn,
she says without a doubt,
"I'm going to be a fashion designer!"
in a confident shout.

Ms. Johnson then speaks as she looks
at her students' faces.
"Your lives are going to take you
to many different places.

"I've taught at this school
for many, many years.
I've seen my students grow up to have
successful careers.

"And though you may be
from a small town,
remember there is talent
spread all around.

"It doesn't matter if you end up
on a stage or basketball team.
Work hard and never, ever
give up on your dreams."

"Even if people say you can't,
or if they don't agree,
never forget that you can be
whatever you want to be.

"When opportunity knocks,
be sure to answer the door.
And just like eagles,
I want you to soar."

With that, the students begin
completing their daily tasks.
Whenever they have questions,
they make sure to ask.

As the school day goes on,
Mia learns more and more.
She keeps wondering with excitement
what the future has in store.

By the time she arrives home,
she is floating on air.
At dinner time,
she cannot wait to share.

Mia raves about her day,
barely touching her plate.
She tells her family all about
how she is destined to be great.

Her family smiles, remembering
the wise words of Ms. Johnson, too.
Then her father says,
"Just know we're always proud of you."

Mia is still floating
as she tries to settle for bed.
Everything Ms. Johnson told the class
dances around her head.

Her mother comes into her room
to tell her "good night."
Mom kisses Mia's forehead
and tucks her in tight.

Then she whispers in her ear
one final reminder.
"Sweet dreams,
my little fashion designer."

About the Author

Kailanya S. Brailey grew up in Livingston, SC. Her family, teachers, and community were the key forces in the collective effort that encouraged her to SOAR and pursue her "GREATER" unapologetically. As a student attending the schools in the small town of North, SC, she increased her love of learning, her confidence as a learner, and her pride in where she was from and who she could become. It did not matter where she was from. North signified where she was and also the direction in which she could go.

As an educator, it became her mission to inspire and empower others with the guiding principles that had been instilled in her in that small town.

Still in South Carolina and currently serving as a school administrator, Kailanya continuously strives to impress upon others the importance of cultivating the drive to keep going, keep striving, and keep growing in the pursuit of learning and realizing your dreams.

CPSIA information can be obtained
at www.ICGtesting.com
Printed in the USA
BVHW020234271120
594323BV00002B/6